STO

FRIENDS
OF ACPL

W9-AGW-486

G

PRAIRIE DOGS IN PRAIRIE DOG TOWN

Prairie Dogs in Prairie Dog Town

By Irmengarde Eberle

Illustrated by John Hamberger

THOMAS Y. CROWELL COMPANY • NEW YORK

BY THE AUTHOR:

Basketful: The Story of Our Foods
Fawn in the Woods
Modern Medical Discoveries
Prairie Dogs in Prairie Dog Town

Library of Congress Cataloging in Publication Data

Eberle, Irmengarde, date
  Prairie dogs in prairie dog town.
SUMMARY: Chronicles life in a prairie dog village showing how a mother raises her litter
and educates them to life in the prairie community.
1. Prairie dogs—Legends and stories. [1. Prairie dogs—Stories] I. Hamberger, John, illus.
II. Title. PZ10.3.E17Pr [Fic] 73-9921 ISBN 0-690-00069-3 ISBN 0-690-00534-2 (lib. bdg.)

1 2 3 4 5 6 7 8 9 10

To
Andrea Grossman

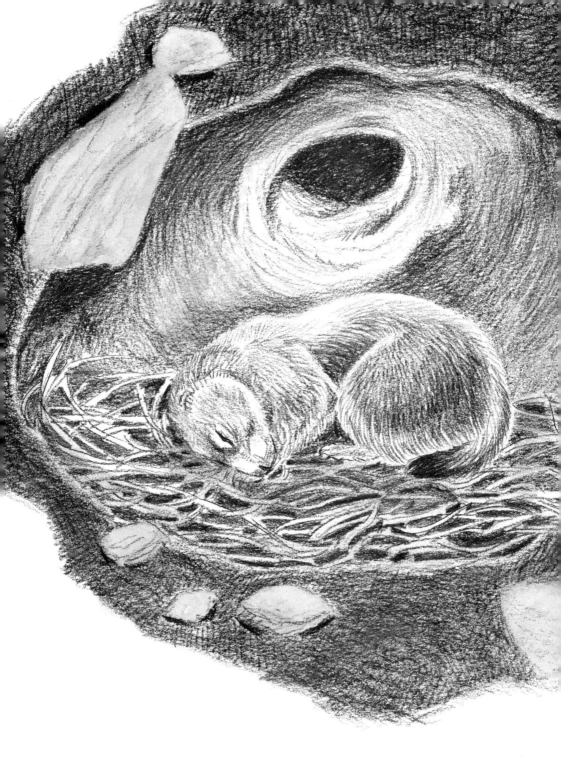

A prairie dog, asleep in her underground home, began to stir. Was it growing faintly warmer? Was a little pale light coming through the darkness around her? Some- how, even here in her nest, five feet below the grass and roots of the upper soil, she could feel a change in the air. Night must be over, and morning on its way.

1

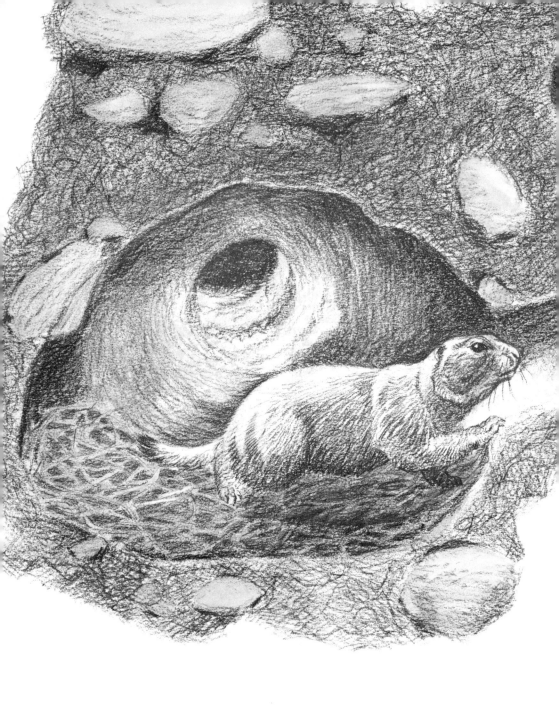

Fully awake now, she was hungry. In the winter months there had been too little food. But now in March many fresh, green plants were springing up, and she could eat all she needed.

Crawling out of her cubbyhole nest she began to move through the dim, and quite narrow, main passage of her burrow. As she went along she made chirring sounds to her two young ones, still with her from last year's litter. Both were in their own small rooms at the ends of short side tunnels, and with beds of dry grass much like hers.

3

Prairie dogs are small animals. The mother weighed about three pounds. These young ones of hers were almost as big as she, but not mature yet. They had the same dark-gray fur with a reddish-brown tinge as hers, and the same short, black-tipped, stubby tails, that they often twitched.

The tunnel along which the mother went was fairly level for a distance of about fourteen feet. Then it turned upward at a sharp slant, and now she saw clear, bright sunlight streaming in at her burrow opening a few feet above. She hurried forward. Two feet or so below the doorway, her passage widened and formed a small side room—it was her listening gallery. Here she stopped, her ears alert. But she heard no sounds of men, badgers, coyotes, or any other enemy. All was quiet. So she went on, and crawled to the top of her earth mound outside. There she sat up on her hind legs.

With her mate's help she had dug herself this fine burrow home last year. Her first set of young ones had been born here, and so would the next litter. The mound she had built up around its opening was important. It was cone-shaped, and so let most of the water of the rains run down its sides and seep into the earth at its base, instead of running into the opening and flooding her burrow. Being over a foot high, the mound was good for a lookout place too.

The mother prairie dog, sitting there now, looked at the other thirty or so mounds that lay around her. They were the homes of her neighbors and relatives who made up this prairie dog town. A few of them were already sticking their heads out of their holes.

Our prairie dog's mate had a home only a few feet from hers. She saw him come out and made chirring sounds of greeting him, which he answered.

Next, the chief prairie dog of the town came out. He was bigger than most and very important. He fought off prairie dogs from another such settlement nearby, and he kept his own group firmly together as a unit.

As the mother sat looking things over in the morning freshness, her big young ones, who had been romping in the passage below, came up behind her. Quickly they ran out to the flat ground and began to tumble about and play there. The mother did not keep her eyes on them long, for they were big enough to look after themselves most of the time.

The sun stood well over the horizon by now—the horizon which lay beyond the miles of plains and rock outcroppings and patches of brush. The prairie dogs could not see the far horizon as people could. They could only see across a few acres, but within that area their vision was sharp and clear.

As more and more of the town's prairie dogs came outdoors they began to mingle. They nuzzled their friends. Some touched each other with open mouths as though kissing. Many made chattering or chirring noises. Or they clicked their teeth and flicked their stubby tails. There was much friendliness. But this play was soon over, for what they all needed now was food.

They began to walk, in their waddling way, across the bare ground which lay between their homes and all around their town's edge for twenty-five feet or more. They kept this area cleared off at all times for, if left alone, the grass and other plants would grow tall and cut off their view. That would never do, for they must be able to see enemies quickly if they came.

The hurrying prairie dogs soon reached the green plants beyond the bare area, and there they scattered and began to nibble the grass. They also bit young, leafy weeds off at their stems and, sitting up, held them in their front paws to eat.

These prairie dogs were in the southwestern part of the Great Plains of the United States. Once there had been many millions of them here, and no doubt far over a billion in all the prairie states together. The prairie dog towns had been bigger then too. As the United States grew in population, railroads were built, and more people settled on the plains year by year. First they developed farms and ranches. Then towns and cities sprang up in many places. This drove millions of prairie dogs from their homes. Thousands died or were killed. Still, millions remained on the less used parts of the plains.

To the ranchers and farmers the little animals were a pest. This was because horses, rounding up cattle, sometimes stumbled into the prairie dog holes and threw their riders off dangerously. Or the horses broke their own legs. And the prairie dogs ate a great deal of the grass— grass that the ranchers wanted for their beef cattle.

Farmers with milk cows did not like the hordes of small grass eaters either. Besides, some of the prairie dogs harmed crops by digging burrows in the fields. So in the 1930s the government began a program of killing them with poison. Some of this was necessary because of the people's needs. But the exterminators overdid it.

Actually, the prairie dogs had been good for the land. Their burrows aired the soil. A little water from the rains always ran into their home holes and so seeped deep into the earth, keeping it moist. Much more ran into the many abandoned burrows where the mounds had been worn down. The water that ran deep below the surface formed pools in underground hollows. Ranchers and townspeople could then get it by digging wells. This was important at all times, but especially during the dry seasons.

Since the millions of prairie dogs had been exterminated, most of this rainwater had been running off into gulleys, creeks, and rivers, and finally was lost in distant lakes or in the ocean. The land became drier, and

12

grass turned brown too quickly in summer. There was less water underground for wells too.

Farmers and ranchers finally became aware of this, but they still did not want prairie dogs back on their land. Then conservationists saw that this kind of mammal was about to be wiped out. So these citizens, and later also the states and the federal government, arranged for the protection of some of the prairie dogs. Soon several of the remaining few were brought into national and state parks in the plains states. Protected there, they have increased, from a half dozen in some places to a few hundred or a few thousand in others. A small scattering have also survived outside the parks, in the stony, less grassy areas where men or cattle seldom go.

13

The members of our prairie dog town were at the edge of one of the state parks—part of a wilderness refuge.

Today, after our mother prairie dog had eaten awhile, she left the pasture and went back to her burrow. Along the way she picked up a mouthful of dry grass and took it with her.

Far underground in her own small twelve-inch-wide room she put it down, and rearranged the dry grass which was already there, making her bed softer and cozier. And there, in a little while, her five young were born.

They were tiny and naked. Their eyelids were shut tight like those of young kittens and many other baby animals. The mother's eyes watched them. After awhile the little ones wanted to suckle, and she lay down on her side so that each could reach a nipple.

Like all prairie dogs the mother did not need to drink water. Because of the juices of the plants she ate, she had enough moisture in her body so that she had plenty of milk for her babies. She stayed close to them for a long time after they fell asleep. She warmed them with her body, and gently touched them with her nose now and then.

Later in the day she went out and hurriedly ate again. When she returned a half hour later, she saw one of her neighbors looking in at her entrance hole. Quickly she made angry noises and chased her away. She would let no one outside her family into her burrow while she had a new litter. Next her mate came by. He too stopped, and he was welcome. Briefly he stood guard at her entrance. He would do that many times now that the babies—his and his mate's—had arrived. Often the mother prairie dog and her year-old young ones joined him there long enough to greet each other.

The mother watched over her tiny babies almost all the time, to make sure that no enemies came near them. She examined her long back tunnel and escape hole that led out behind a big rock. She must make sure it remained open. She seldom needed it—but she must be sure that she could take the babies out that secret way if an enemy came in the front entrance.

The little ones grew quite fast, and in a few days fine, soft fur covered their naked bodies. Two weeks later their eyes opened. Now they became playful. They nibbled and bumped each other in the nest, and tumbled about.

Most days the mother found everything peaceful outside when she went to eat. A few lizards, including horned toads, ran around, mixing with her and her neighbors. They were harmless, and were a natural part of the scene. But before long a few upsetting things happened.

18

First a burrowing owl came to the town. All the prairie dogs made a great fuss and tried to chase him away, for owls like this one eat very young prairie dogs if they can get at them.

The owl would not leave but made himself at home in an abandoned burrow. The prairie dogs barked and chattered around this place for a long time. Finally they gave up and let him stay. But they watched him. And any prairie dog who saw him go to one of the burrows where there was a litter, barked loudly. Then several ran at him to chase him away. They bit at his feathers and clawed at him, and they bumped him with their noses and foreheads till he went back to his own place. He would catch himself some meadow mice later on. That would still his hunger.

Another time, late in the afternoon, a great hawk flew high over the nibbling prairie dogs in the grass. He was more dangerous, for he would eat any one of them he could catch—adults or babies.

The first one who saw the big bird's shadow slide over the grass, sat up quickly and barked to warn his neighbors. Most of the others barked then too, and ran to their homes or into the nearest burrow they could reach.

The chief of the town and several other males and females paused on top of their mounds. From there they again barked sharply to hurry the last prairie dogs along. Then they too slipped quickly into their home holes.

All these barks had been of a special tone that meant that the danger was coming from the air.

Our prairie dog mother and her last year's young ones had dropped into their home hole very quickly. Now she stopped and sat in the listening room, waiting.

The hawk had been far up in the air when his shadow
fell on the town's food patch. By the time he had dropped
down to grab one of them with his open claws, the land
was empty. Every prairie dog had vanished into the
earth. The hawk, disappointed, soared over the place for
a few minutes, searching for them. Finally he gave up
and flew off.

24

There was a short silence. No one stirred. After a while the chief prairie dog and a few others stuck their heads out guardedly and looked about. Seeing nothing of the hawk, they gave a songlike bark that meant, "All is clear and safe." As usual, the others came out at that. They looked, listened, and hurried off to eat as before.

But more trouble soon came. One day while the father of our prairie dog family was some distance from his home, a five-foot-long rattlesnake came gliding toward his burrow. Again special barks of danger arose from the prairie dogs who saw it. These signals told that the danger was on the ground. Perhaps it even told what kind of danger it was. For instead of dropping down their holes, the chief prairie dog and several others gathered around the rattler and scolded. They were trying to make it leave. But the rattler went right on, and soon slid into the burrow. There it stayed.

The crowd of prairie dogs grew more and more upset.

The snake could not eat full-grown prairie dogs. Like the owl, it had come there to dine on the town's newborn in the burrows. It would not find any in this one because the burrow belonged to a male. But left alone, the snake would soon come out and find babies elsewhere.

Quick action was called for. A number of the prairie dogs began to claw at the mound and push the loosened earth into the opening of the burrow where the snake was. The father prairie dog, owner of the burrow, worked at it as hard as any of them. Together they hurriedly closed up the entrance hole.

Other prairie dog helpers went around to the escape hole of the burrow, thirty feet away. In a few minutes that was plugged solidly too, and the big, dangerous snake was trapped inside! It would die there in time, from lack of air and food. It would never harm a small, helpless prairie dog from this day on.

But now our father prairie dog was homeless. There was only one thing he could do. He turned away and began to look for a place to dig himself a new home. He found a nearby spot that suited him. It was far enough from his mate's and the other burrows so that he would not run his tunnel into theirs. He started scratching at the soil. His mate came and helped him for a while. When she had to leave to go to her babies, a neighbor

helped him. They dug energetically, taking turns. The earth flew, and the beginning of a new burrow took shape.

The father slept in a nearby abandoned tunnel that night. The next day, and many days more, he worked to make the tunnel reach farther underground. Then, he made his nest cubbyhole, his escape exit, and finally his listening room near the front entrance.

For our mother prairie dog and pups, things went on much as usual. Her last year's young ones sometimes went into their father's burrow to see what was going on. Or they helped him dig a little—but they were not of much help yet.

Meanwhile, in the mother prairie dog's home the youngest babies began to drink less of her milk. One day they stopped entirely. She looked them over. It was clear that the sturdy, small creatures needed green food now. So she made sounds at them. They understood they were to follow her, and she led them along the tunnel toward the front.

In a few minutes the young ones found themselves in the great outside world for the first time.

How bright it was! And how wide the world lay all around them. Best to keep close to their mother. So they did, and went with her to the edge of the nibbling grounds. Soon they got quite used to being outside. They ate a little, and often stopped and just played with each other and with other small young ones that happened by.

Toward evening, when the sun was low over the horizon, the prairie dogs, young and old, had had enough food, and they began to go back to their homes for the night. Many of the adults then stretched themselves out flat on top of their mounds for a while. There they relaxed in the mild evening light.

Many an evening our prairie dog mother, and her older young ones and her babies, did this too. But by the time darkness fell they, like all the other members of the

34

town, had dropped down their tunnels. As night came, all slept.

One very hot afternoon, dark storm clouds gathered in the northwest. Lightning flashed and thunder cracked and rolled. Slowly the clouds pushed onward until they were right overhead. A few big drops of rain fell, and before all the prairie dogs could flee, the storm broke loose in a great torrent of rain. The last ones into their homes got soaking wet.

35

Inside her own burrow our prairie dog mother let her young ones go below to the nests. She herself stayed in her listening gallery, from where she could watch the storm. She must see what would happen next. And then, before her eyes, the protective mound around her entrance gave way under the rush of rain. Immediately the water ran into her tunnel. Wet and frantic, she outran the water in her passageway to get to her young ones. Far back there, she found them still safe and dry. But they had sensed danger and were cowering at one side. She tried to comfort them. She nosed and sniffed them.

But she would not rest with them long. She must see if there was danger from the direction of her escape tunnel. She hurried along the back passage. Yes, some water was coming in there—but it was not too bad yet. She returned to her young ones and crouched with them a little while.

Gradually she became aware that the noise of the thunder was lessening. The storm was passing on. She ran up front again to take a look there. Less water was running in now. And the dry, thirsty earth had already soaked up most of the earlier flow. This was good. She went on upward.

36

Once outside she saw that there was truly little left of the important protective mound around her entrance. She looked about her and saw her mate already at work. His new burrow had had its mound washed away too. And all around the town other prairie dogs were coming out to repair theirs. She set to work too, clawing and kicking the wet earth upward to put her mound in shape again. Her two older young ones came and helped, and they were beginning to be of real use now.

37

For some days after this the prairie dog town lay in summer quiet and peace. Many years ago there would have been badgers, coyotes, and ferrets visiting the town in search of prairie dogs to eat. But since so many millions of the small animals had been exterminated by people, most ferrets had died off for lack of food. There were fewer badgers too, and almost no coyotes.

The coyotes were gone because the same kind of people who had killed off prairie dogs—the farmers and ranchers—disliked coyotes too. For these animals of the wolf family sometimes attacked and killed young calves and sheep out on the range. Sometimes this meant losses to these men. So they trapped, poisoned, or shot all the coyotes they could. The government people finally helped them by starting a full program of coyote extermination. A bounty was paid for the hides, using these as proof that the animals had actually been done away with.

By the 1960s many people realized that the coyotes had been of great value because they had kept down the mouse and rat population for the farmers. They were an

38

important part of the balance of nature. Now that the coyotes were almost gone, the mice of the prairies, and other rodents, were multiplying by the millions and were destroying great quantities of valuable grain—grain that was needed as food for cattle, pigs, and chickens.

The state governments and the people who owned ranches and farms tried to get together on this new problem. Still some insisted on going on killing coyotes. Other men wanted to begin to protect the few that were still alive, and so give them a chance to increase at least a little. They wanted them to eat the rats and mice of the plains.

The subject was talked about, and written about in farm papers and magazines. But not much was done. However, some farmers and ranchmen did begin on their own to protect coyotes. They put up signs on their land forbidding hunters to shoot or trap or poison coyotes there. A few of these animals survived in state and national parks.

The coyotes were, however, the great enemies of prairie dogs. Coyotes are meat eaters, and prairie dogs are good food for them.

In the rolling hills to the west of our prairie dog town a few coyotes had come to live among the rocks and brush. Often at night their howls and barks rang far and wide across the country.

Sometimes a lone coyote would call to his mate. An answer would come, and they would trot in each other's direction until they met. Or the coyote pair would howl and yip to get one or two others to join them on a hunting trip. The small group would trot along together then, looking for mice, rats, jackrabbits, and cottontails. Or, among the bushes, they might catch a fawn, if they saw one that was separated from its strong, grown-up deer mother.

This spring a coyote pair had had young ones in their den. The pups grew and were weaned. They needed meat such as their parents ate. So the mother and father hunted more than ever.

Roaming far from their den one clear, moonlit night, the two came upon the prairie dog village. But as all the small animals were asleep far underground, the coyotes could not find a single one to catch. They sniffed about and then trotted on. But they did not forget the place. They would come here again by daylight sometime.

The prairie dogs in their town did not know that coyotes had been here.

During the daytime our mother prairie dog went contentedly about her business of caring for her little ones and eating. She watched her healthy, growing babies nibble and play. Often she chattered at the father, and he came and ate with his family.

The days grew warmer. Grasshoppers, beetles, and cutworms appeared, and they too were good food. It was a change from the plant diet.

The whole town had been feeding on the vegetation on the east side for quite a while. The low plants were almost nibbled away. So one day all the prairie dogs turned to the west side and began to eat there. In this way they gave the old feeding grounds a chance to grow up again.

The days grew still hotter with the coming of midsummer. When the great heat of the noonday sun beat down on their small, furry backs, most of the prairie dogs stopped eating and went back home. There, deep in their cool tunnels, they stayed until the sun was lower in the west and its rays more gentle.

For several weeks our prairie dog mother and her new pups and two large grown young ones got along fine. By now the youngest pups ate almost as much as adult prairie dogs. And they learned new things day by day. They learned to be alert like their mother and father. They learned the meanings of all the different kinds of barks and chirrs and clicks their parents and neighbors made. Soon they could tell when an enemy came stalking them along the ground, and when a hawk or eagle was about to attack from the sky. They knew the safety sounds, so different from the friendly sounds of neighbors and parents.

Their home area became a lively place in midsummer. Not only were all the prairie dogs and their young outside many hours every day, but there were more and more cottontails and jackrabbits around, and some odd, long-legged birds called roadrunners. Small, trim lizards flicked their tongues and caught insects. Like the burrowing owl, grasshopper mice had taken over some of the abandoned burrows. They made nests of dry grass inside and plugged the openings with more of it. They left only a small hole, no bigger than their own bodies, so that they could live as secretly as possible and, again and again, have new litters of young.

Many birds, small and friendly, flitted through the air above the prairie dog town—sparrows, catbirds, buntings, and killdeer. Often some of them came down among the prairie dogs and ate with them, choosing plant seeds and insects.

The prairie dogs knew all these creatures. But they were unaware of the coyotes in the hills.

The coyote pair that had come to the prairie dog town weeks ago were having a busy time. Their four pups were getting hungrier every day as they grew. Both father and mother worked almost continually to keep them fed. They preferred to work in the darkness, but they often had to hunt in the daytime too. They took only brief periods of rest. They were as good parents to their young as the prairie dogs were to theirs.

Late one afternoon the father coyote left his mate to guard near the den and went to join another male coyote to hunt farther away. Together the two set out for the prairie dog village.

At first they ran swiftly, but as they came within sight of the group of prairie dog mounds they slowed down and walked quietly. They wanted to take the animals by surprise.

It was about four in the afternoon, and a few of the prairie dogs were coming out for their late afternoon's nibbling. The coyotes saw them from far off. They separated and, hidden by rocks, high grass, and weeds, crept forward, each from a different side. They stood still a moment and waited until more of the animals had come out. Then, as if by a signal to each other, they leaped forward and raced into the open to cut the prairie dogs off from their burrows.

The prairie dogs heard and saw them almost at the instant that the coyotes started toward them. Several let out their usual barks of warning, and all ran to find the nearest place of safety. Some reached their own homes. Stopping a moment on the mounds of their holes, they urged everyone else to hurry in.

One coyote saw the bold chief of the town on his mound and ran to nab him. Instantly the chief dropped into his hole, and was four feet down and safe.

Here and there other prairie dogs ran into each other's burrows. One dashed into the owl's place and got a sharp peck.

Our mother prairie dog's older offspring took care of themselves. They had run into their father's home, as that was nearest at the moment. The mother and her smallest ones were farther from a mound. So she hurried them along to the nearest small hole—which was her own escape hole behind the big rock. She pushed the young ones with her nose to hurry them.

At last she had them all inside her burrow. In her nest room she settled them quickly. Then she hurried forward to her listening gallery to see if she could learn what was going on outside.

She heard screams from above. One or more of the prairie dogs had been caught by the coyotes. Her heart beat fast. She waited until the cries stopped. Then she went up a little farther and looked out warily.

There was nothing to see close by, and a strange, frightening silence had fallen over the town. Even the friendly birds, lizards, and rabbits had fled from the coyotes.

The mother came out further and, from the top of her mound, saw the two big animals trotting up the hill, each with something grayish in his mouth.

She sat on her hind legs and looked and waited. The leader of the town was already out. In a moment he gave an all-clear bark and a few chirrs. And he threw his forelegs up so vigorously that he toppled over backward. Quickly he righted himself and barked again. As usual, others came up on their mounds and helped bark and chirr, and some clicked their teeth.

Then our mother prairie dog made sounds too, calling her youngest ones to come to her. Slowly they came crawling up. Soon the other prairie dogs of the town came out, sat upright, and listened and watched. Gradually all relaxed and went to eat again.

Two members of the close-knit little community were gone. But the town quickly got used to their absence. One had been a female with young ones, but fortunately they were old enough to take care of themselves fairly well.

Our mother prairie dog watched her young more carefully than ever for a while. Then she too forgot about the fearful happening, and life went on as usual.

The coyotes came again one morning. But the chief prairie dog saw them at a distance this time, and warned the others quickly. And this time they were able to slip away into the many holes before the big animals could catch any of them. All were safe.

The coyotes looked around, sniffed, then scratched a few of the grasshopper mice from their nests in the old burrows and ate them. Then, hurriedly, they went off to find more game perhaps bigger than prairie dogs.

The summer passed. September was still hot, but when October came the days were often cooler, and then the prairie dogs began to molt. As their summer fur fell out, they grew warmer, thicker fur for the cold days of the brief winter that lay ahead.

For a while the prairie dog mother and father still found enough green plants for themselves and their family. But soon most of the grass became brown and dry. Then the prairie dogs dug up roots to eat. They clawed up low cactus plants too and, avoiding their spiky thorns, ate the soft, juicy insides.

Often cold winds blew. And one evening snow began to fall. It made a chilly cover over the earth. But the prairie dogs were snug and warm underground in their nests. It snowed long into the night.

The next morning when the prairie dog mother and
her five young ones—now quite big—started out to look
for food, they found their exit hole blocked with snow.
The mother scratched some of it away. From outside she
heard more scratching. It was her mate helping her clear
her passage.

In a little while the mother and her big young ones
came out. They and the father prairie dog made friendly
chirring sounds at each other as usual. Then all went off
together over the white, cold earth. They dug up roots
and bits of cactus again. Only a few neighbors joined
them. Our prairie dog family did not stay out long, for
their paws began to hurt from the snow.

Several more storms of snow or sleet came that winter, but in between there were often mild days. In the pleasant sunshine the snow and sleet often melted quickly, and then every prairie dog in the town came out. But all winter they were always a little hungry, for there was too little food, even when they dug hard and long. With the passing months they grew thin and restless.

Late in January the father prairie dog came into the mother's burrow and stayed for some days. Inside or outside, the whole family was almost always together now. During these days the mother and father mated. And in the mother's body young ones began to grow again. After a while the father went back to his own burrow close by.

Now the two older young ones, born two years ago, were truly grown up. Some young males from other

families came to them and sniffed and nuzzled them. Soon they became pairs, and then the young females went away with their males to start homes of their own in new places.

In March the mother in the old home burrow gave birth to a litter of six new, little pups.

Spring came slowly, turning the earth green again. Once more the prairie dog mother and her family and neighbors were outdoors much of the time. With food bountiful they became plump and content as before.

A few of the young mature males and females of the town went a short distance away and started a village of their own. It was like a suburb of the old town. There the young males fought a little among themselves. The winner—the strongest one—became the chief prairie dog of the new colony.

In the old town the mother, with her new young ones, again spent the good, warm days out in the open with her mate and the many other prairie dogs.

They lived peacefully most of the time. Yet they kept their ears and eyes open in case a rattlesnake, a burrowing owl, or, worst of all, coyotes, hawks, or a man should come that way.

The youngest ones, like those born before them, learned how to look out for themselves, and often barked for the safety of all. They grew up surrounded by family and neighbors, helpful and friendly with each other.

About the Author

Irmengarde Eberle is the author of more than 65 books for young readers, in both fiction and nonfiction categories; many of her books have won awards and prizes and have been published in countries throughout the world.

Ms. Eberle grew up in Texas, where she graduated from Texas Woman's University. Migrating to New York, she embarked on a career in textile design. When her interest in nature stories led to the publication of her first book for children, *Hop, Skip and Fly*—an instant and long-lasting success—she turned her full attention to writing.

For many years she was chairman of the Children's Book Section of the Authors' Guild, which she helped establish. She and her husband, Arnold Koehler, have traveled widely; they make their home in New York City.

About the Artist

John Hamberger has illustrated more than a score of outstanding children's books about animals and nature, including his own picture books. He is a member of the Society of Animal Artists, and he has a permanent exhibition of paintings in the American Museum of Natural History. Mr. Hamberger divides his time between a farm in Camptown, Pennsylvania, and a home in New York City.